I Love to Sing

For my brother 'Fred'.

First published in hardback by
Scholastic Australia in 2008
First published in paperback in Great Britain
by HarperCollins Children's Books in 2010

10 9 8 7 6 5 4 3 2 1

ISBN-13: 978-0-00-730920-7

HarperCollins Children's Books is a division of
HarperCollins Publishers Ltd.

A CIP catalogue record for this title is available from
the British Library.

Visit our website at www.harpercollins.co.uk

Printed in China

by Anna Walker

HarperCollins *Children's Books*

My name is Ollie.

I love to sing.

I love to sing
on my chair.

I love to sing
on my stair.

I love to sing in the rain

and the sun.

and with my brother,
just for fun.

I love to sing with ducks

in the park.

I sing with Fred,

who loves to bark!

I love to sing

in the lemon tree

and in my bath
with a cup of tea.

But what I love best
is to sing in bed-
a happy song
for me and Fred!